For Zoe Kennedy,
a girl of great determination and drive,
with love and admiration – IW

For Daddy bear, Mommy bear,
Sime and K-dog – OV

© The Chicken House 2002

Text © Ian Whybrow 2002
Illustrations © Olivia Villet 2002

First published in the United Kingdom in 2002 by
The Chicken House, 2 Palmer Street, Frome, Somerset, BA11 1DS

Printed and bound U.A.E.

British Library Cataloguing in Publication Data available.
Library of Congress Cataloguing in Publication data available.

ISBN: 1 903434 55 6

SISSY BUTTONS
Takes Charge!

Ian Whybrow
Illustrated by Olivia Villet

The Chicken HOUSE

From the time she could talk, Cecelia Beaton liked buttons. That's why, when people asked her name, she liked to answer, "Sissy Buttons." She loved teddy bears, picnics and big machines and there was nothing Sissy Buttons couldn't do if she tried.

Only, when it came to tidying up,
Sissy Buttons always felt too tired.

One summer evening, quite late, her mum said: "Five minutes to tidy up before supper time, Sissy Buttons!" "Oh Mum," said Sissy Buttons,"Can you do it? I'm too tired."

So Mum put her hands on her hips and she said, "Now watch me very carefully and listen to what I say:

Just button up your buttons,
And look up in the sky.
Then say, 'There's nothing I can't do
If I just try and try.' "

"Hmm," said Sissy Buttons, and lay
down to think while the sun began to set.

Soon she was dreaming of bears
and picnics and big machines.
And as she dreamed, she heard her teds talking.

"Wouldn't it be nice to have a picnic in
the woods?" said Sailor, the tumbling ted.
"But how do we do that?" said Teasy Ted.
"Let's ask Sissy Buttons if she knows
what to do," said Squeezy Ted.

So they woke her up and asked her.

"That's easy," said Sissy Buttons.

Quick as quick, she picked up all the picnic things and popped them into the bucket of the big yellow digger and off they went to the woods. But when they got there the teds did what bears usually do.

They didn't know how to help ...

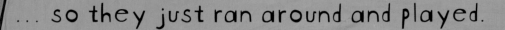

... so they just ran around and played.

Well, Sissy Buttons spread out the blanket.

And Sissy Buttons put out the plates.

Sailor, the tumbling ted, kept falling over.
It was Sailor who squished the cake.

UH-OH!

Then Teasy Ted got a long grass and tickled Squeezy Ted. Down went the lemonade, all over the blanket.

Shame!

Then all the teds got tired and upset.
They put in their thumbs.
And went Num Num.

And Teasy Ted said, "Sailor sat on the cake and
I made Squeezy Ted knock over the lemonade.
Sorry, Sissy, can you help? We can't do anything!"

"You can if you try," said Sissy Buttons,
as she put her hands on her hips.
"Now watch me very carefully,
and listen to what I say:

I button up my buttons,
And look up in the sky.
I say, 'There's nothing I can't do
If I just try and try.' "

And so Sissy Buttons took charge!

She gathered up all the teds in the bucket of her big yellow digger and off she bumped with them down to the lake.

UP went the bucket.

Then **DOWN** went the bucket.

And **INTO** the water tumbled Sailor and Teasy Ted and Squeezy Ted.

SHLOOSH!

"This is nice!" said Sailor Ted.

"I can splash you!" said Teasy Ted.

"I feel wide awake!" said Squeezy Ted.

They were having a lovely time after all!

Sissy Buttons smiled. Then she ...

Unbuttoned all her buttons,
And looked up in the sky.
She said: "There's nothing **I** can't do
If **I** just try and try."

As the sun went down,
Sissy Buttons did Front Swim,

Back Swim,

Side Swim

and Duck Dive.

"Gosh, Sissy Buttons," said the teds.
"Is there anything you can't do?"

"Just remember: buttons, sky, do, try,"
said Sissy Buttons.

"Now, who's ready for a sausage on a stick?"
"Me, me, me!" said the teds.

What a laugh they had, bumping back to the picnic place.

When they got there, the teds said
to Sissy Buttons, "Is this right?

We button up our buttons,
And look up in the sky.
We say, 'There's nothing we can't do
If we just try and try!' "

And then the teds took charge!

In two shakes, what did the three teds do?
They did everything!

They built a beautiful bonfire.
They made creamy cups of cocoa!
They did buttery spuds in their jackets!
They did sizzling sausages on sticks!

Succulent!

"Have you tidied up yet?" called Mum.

"Come and see!" said Sissy Buttons.

"What a beautiful job!" said Mum. "And you'll never guess what we're having for supper ... sausages on sticks!"

"Succulent!" said Sissy Buttons.

"Buttons, sky, do, try!" said the teds.